Oxford University Press, Walton Street, Oxford OX2 6DP

Oxford New York Toronto
Delhi Bombay Calcutta Madras Karachi
Kuala Lumpur Singapore Hong Kong Tokyo
Nairobi Dar es Salaam Cape Town
Melbourne Auckland Madrid

and associated companies in
Berlin Ibadan

Oxford is a trade mark of Oxford University Press

A CIP catalogue record for this book is available
from the British Library

ISBN 0 19 279908 8 (hardback)
ISBN 0 19 272280 8 (paperback)

Printed in Hong Kong

THE
Three
Billy-Goats
Gruff
Val Biro

Oxford University Press

Once upon a time there were three Billy-Goats.
The smallest one was called Little Billy-Goat Gruff.

The middle-sized one was
Middle Billy-Goat Gruff.

And the biggest one was Big Billy-Goat Gruff.

They all lived together on a mountainside.
It was fine for skipping about,
but so full of stones that
there was very little grass to eat.

So the three Billy-Goats Gruff
were thin and hungry.

One day Little Billy-Goat Gruff looked across the valley.
'There is a lovely green grass meadow on the other side,'
he said. 'Let's go there and make ourselves fat.'

So the three Billy-Goats Gruff
decided to go to the green grass meadow.
But first they had to cross a bridge.

Now, under that rickety bridge
there lived a Troll.
A horrible Troll with eyes like
saucers and a nose like
a knobbly carrot.

'This bridge is MY bridge,'
he growled. 'I shall gobble
up anyone who tries to
cross it.'

Little Billy-Goat Gruff
didn't know about the Troll,
and he tripped merrily down
the mountainside to cross the bridge.

Trippety-trip, went the
rickety bridge.

'WHO'S THAT tripping over MY bridge?'
roared the Troll.

'It's only me,' said Little Billy-Goat Gruff
in a little voice.

'Then I'm coming to gobble you up!'
yelled the Troll from under the bridge.

'Oh, please don't eat me, I'm much too
small,' said Little Billy-Goat Gruff.
'There's another Billy-Goat coming along
behind me, who is much bigger.'

The horrible Troll hummed and
hawed, but in the end he let the
Little Billy-Goat Gruff go to
the green grass meadow.

Soon, Middle Billy-Goat Gruff came trotting down the mountainside to cross the bridge.

Trottery-trot, went the rickety bridge.

'WHO'S THAT trotting over MY bridge?' roared the Troll.

'It's only me,' said Middle Billy-Goat Gruff in a middling voice.

'Then I'm coming to gobble you up!' yelled the Troll, and leaned upon the bridge.

'Please don't eat me,' said Middle Billy-Goat Gruff. 'Wait till you see the third Billy-Goat. He's *really* big! He'll make a much better dinner.'

The horrible Troll hummed and
hawed, hawed and hummed, but he
let Middle Billy-Goat Gruff go, too.

And then came Big Billy-Goat Gruff,
trampling down the mountainside to cross the bridge.

Trampety-tramp, went the rickety bridge.

'WHO'S THAT trampling over MY bridge?'
roared the Troll.
'It's ME,' said Big Billy-Goat Gruff
in a big gruff voice.

'Then I'm coming to
gobble you up right NOW!' yelled
the Troll, and jumped on to the bridge.

But Big Billy-Goat Gruff
put down his horned head and said:

'You won't eat me, it's no good trying,
My two big horns will send you flying!'

And with that he charged at the Troll,
who turned in fright to run away.
Big Billy-Goat Gruff
tossed his horned head and . . .

. . . the horrible Troll flew
right up into the air
    SWOOOSH
and fell down into the river
    SPLLLASH!
And he was never seen again.

Big Billy-Goat Gruff crossed over
the bridge, *trampety-tramp*,
and joined the other two Billy-Goats
Gruff in the green grass meadow.

And there they all stayed and made
themselves fat on the lovely grass.

Ever since that day, the three Billy-Goats Gruff can
cross over the rickety bridge whenever they like.
Only they've grown so fat on the green grass that
now they can hardly walk home!